For Beck

Copyright © 2021 by Andrew Joyner

All rights reserved. Published in the United States by Random House Studio,
an imprint of Random House Children's Books,
a division of Penguin Random House LLC, New York.

Random House Studio and the colophon are registered trademarks of
Penguin Random House LLC.

Visit us on the Web! rhcbooks.com

Educators and librarians, for a variety of teaching tools, visit us at RHTeachersLibrarians.com

Library of Congress Cataloging-in-Publication Data is available upon request.
ISBN 978-0-593-37518-1 (trade) — ISBN 978-0-593-37520-4 (lib. bdg.)
ISBN 978-0-593-37519-8 (ebook)

The artist used Procreate to create the illustrations for this book.
The text of this book is set in 24-point Adobe Caslon Pro Regular.
Interior design by Rachael Cole

MANUFACTURED IN CHINA
10 9 8 7 6 5 4 3 2 1
First Edition

LOVE was INSIDE

by Andrew Joyner

RANDOM HOUSE STUDIO 🏠 NEW YORK

Who was inside?

I was inside.

I was inside my room with a clock

and my dog

and a picture of Nan.

I sat at my desk and went to school.

I saw my friends
and Ms. Gomez.

They were
inside too.

Everyone was inside.

Here was inside.

There was inside.

Families were inside.

Nan was inside.

A song was inside.

Breakfast was inside.

Lunch was inside.

Dinner was inside.

I put too much pizza inside.

A day was inside.

Then a night was inside.

A week has seven days
and nights, all inside.

Monday

Tuesday

Wednesday

Thursday

Friday

Saturday

Sunday

I stayed inside.

There were days
I felt sad inside.

And sometimes scared
and mad inside.

So I dreamed of a day
when I would open the door.

I would jump
down the steps

and run up
the street

and across two blocks . . .

. . . to eat pizza with Nan.

Everyone would be outside.

A game would be outside.

All my friends
would be outside.

Even Ms. Gomez
would be outside.

I would be outside!

But I know I will always remember . . .

. . . the days we stayed inside.

When I was strong inside.
When I was brave inside.

When love was inside.

Remember when you were inside?

Tell your own inside story
on a piece of paper
or make your own book.

Here are some questions to get you started.

Who was inside with you?

What did you miss most?

What did being inside give
you more time to do?

What did you learn when
you were inside?

Don't forget to include drawings
of what you did inside.